Izzie: Book Two

TRONGATE
FURY

BUDGE WILSON

Izzie: Book Two
TRONGATE
FURY

BUDGE WILSON

PENGUIN
CANADA

PENGUIN CANADA

Published by the Penguin Group

Penguin Group (Canada), 10 Alcorn Avenue, Toronto, Ontario, Canada M4V 3B2
(a division of Pearson Penguin Canada Inc.)

Penguin Group (USA) Inc., 375 Hudson Street, New York, New York 10014, U.S.A.
Penguin Books Ltd, 80 Strand, London WC2R 0RL, England
Penguin Ireland, 25 St Stephen's Green, Dublin 2, Ireland (a division of Penguin Books Ltd)
Penguin Group (Australia), 250 Camberwell Road, Camberwell, Victoria 3124, Australia
(a division of Pearson Australia Group Pty Ltd)
Penguin Books India Pvt Ltd, 11 Community Centre, Panchsheel Park, New Delhi – 110 017, India
Penguin Group (NZ), Cnr Airborne and Rosedale Roads, Albany, Auckland, New Zealand
(a division of Pearson New Zealand Ltd)
Penguin Books (South Africa) (Pty) Ltd, 24 Sturdee Avenue, Rosebank, Johannesburg 2196,
South Africa

Penguin Books Ltd, Registered Offices: 80 Strand, London WC2R 0RL, England

First published 2005

1 2 3 4 5 6 7 8 9 10   (WEB)

Copyright © Budge Wilson, 2005
Cover illustration © Greg Banning, 2005
Full-page and chapter-opener illustrations © Heather Collins, 2005
Design: Matthews Communications Design Inc.
Map © Sharon Matthews

*Publisher's note: This book is a work of fiction. Names, characters, places, and incidents either
are the product of the author's imagination or are used fictitiously, and any resemblance
to actual persons living or dead, events, or locales is entirely coincidental.*

Manufactured in Canada.

LIBRARY AND ARCHIVES CANADA CATALOGUING IN PUBLICATION

Wilson, Budge
Izzie : Trongate fury / Budge Wilson.

(Our Canadian girl)
"Izzie: Book Two".
ISBN 0-14-301465-X

I. Title. II. Title: Trongate fury. III. Series.

PS8595.I5813I995   2005   jC813'.54   C2004-905412-0

Visit the Penguin Group (Canada) website at **www.penguin.ca**

To my friend
Joan Tregunno
who saw it all

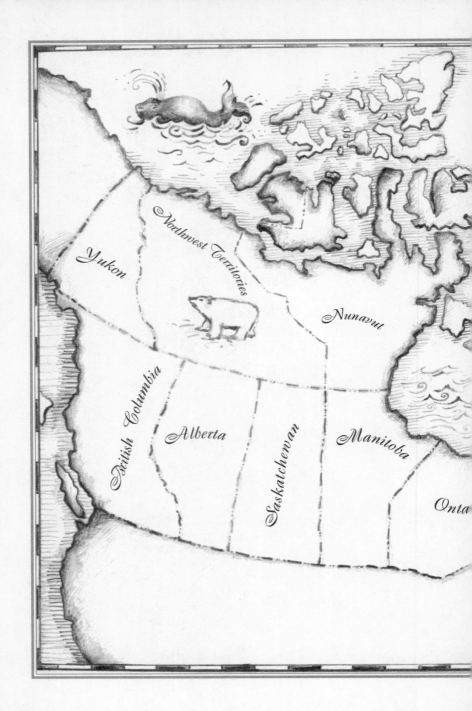

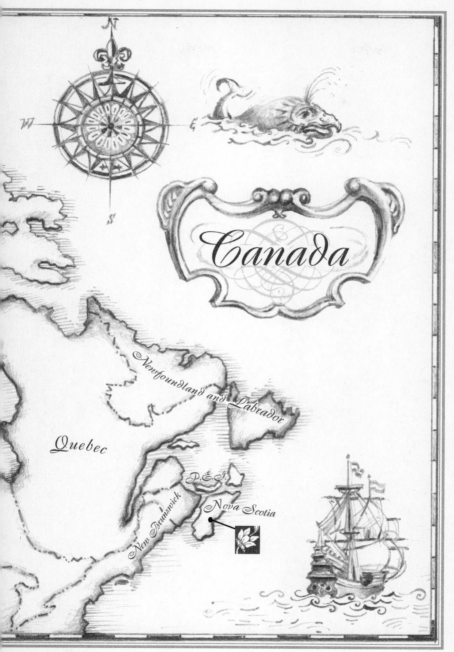

 Marks the location of the story

CHANGES

O NLY TWO WEEKS have passed since the ferocious storm swept Nova Scotia. It is now 1942, but for the Publicover family, everything has remained much the same.

In 1941, Mr. Publicover had tried to enlist in the navy but was turned down because he was too old—thirty-seven—and because he had a family to support. This was a big disappointment for him and a huge relief for his wife and children.

But the war is still raging in Europe: gas and fuel rationing continues; fears about the enemy submarines lurking outside Halifax Harbour remain; and the newspapers carry unwelcome information about casualties and death on the battlefields and on the open seas. But none of this is new.

However, changes are taking place in Canada that will have a large impact on its citizens. Before the war started, very few married women worked outside the home. But now, as more and more men go off to war, new labour is needed on farms, in factories, and in places of business.

For the first time, hundreds of women are leaving their homes, venturing forth into a wider world to do the work that men have left behind. Many women, for instance, will be building the corvettes that are so badly needed for the Atlantic convoys. Doing this type of work that is both important and interesting will change the lives of some women forever. Many will become less satisfied with an existence that is fenced in by cooking, laundry, child care, and housecleaning.

For children, changes in their lives will occur with the arrival of many "guest children" from England. Worried about the safety of their children during the horrendous bombing raids on English cities, many parents have sent their children across the Atlantic to live in Canada and elsewhere.

These guest children have customs, speech patterns and accents, war experiences, and educations that differ greatly from those of their new Canadian friends. The results of this small invasion of British children into the homes and schools of Canadians will have intense and long-lasting consequences for the children whom the guests meet and with whom they live.

For Izzie and her family, life hasn't changed much yet. However, on this particular day, Izzie has been feeling uneasy. There was a full moon last night, and she had a strange sense of foreboding when she woke up in the morning. In Nova Scotia—even in 1942—people are often superstitious about a full moon. When the big orange sphere appears on the horizon, it is said that dogs howl, cats wander, and sometimes human tempers flare and nerves get twitchy. Some people have an odd sensation that something awful is about to happen. That's what Izzie has been feeling all morning.

CHAPTER № 1

"When I woke up this morning," said Izzie, "I was sure that something awful was going to happen."

She and Jasper had left their houses in the fishing village of Granite Cove and were walking along the beach in their snow boots, kicking at pieces of frozen seaweed, loosening them from their hold on the sand. Sometimes they stopped to skip stones across the water, when they found ones that were flat enough. Jasper looked at Izzie, puzzled. They had been best friends since before they could walk, but he still often found her hard to figure out.

"What on earth are you talking about?" he said, his brows screwed together. "Why would you think a thing like that?"

The sea was so calm that it looked like a big lake. They could actually see trees reflected in the water off Squid Point—something that almost never happened. It was warm for January—just a bit below freezing—and the sun was shining down on them from a cloudless sky. Jasper often had a way of looking on the gloomy side of things, but right now, the only word he could think of to describe the day was *perfect*. Besides, Izzie had a big grin spread all over her face.

She laughed. "Because there was a full moon last night. People sometimes do weird things during a full moon. They can get just a little bit crazy. Even cats. Adella cries to go out at full-moon time so she can roam through the woods and slaughter things all night."

Jasper's eyebrows were still drawn together. "So what's the awful thing?"

Izzie laughed again. "A great big nothing! How wrong could I be? It just shows how superstitious I am about all that moon stuff. And how dumb. Full moons are so beautiful. Did you see it come up last night over Shag Island, like a giant orange pumpkin? And nothing bad happened. Stupid me."

Jasper was grinning now. "It's so perfect this afternoon that it's hard to believe there's a war on, and that out there—and not so far away," he pointed at the horizon, "people are trying to kill each other." He shook his head.

"And *wanting* to," said Izzie. "The Eisner twins in grade eleven can hardly wait to be eighteen, so they can join the army or navy and go out there and get themselves blown to pieces."

Jasper looked sideways at Izzie. "Well," he said in a low voice, "if I absolutely *had* to go to war, I'd choose the air force. Imagine flipping around in one of those dandy little Spitfire fighter planes, zapping a big bomber out of the sky and sending it crashing to the ground." Jasper was zooming around on the sand, with his arms spread out on each side. He drew his arms together to aim his imaginary gun at the imaginary bomber. "Yes, sir," he sighed. "That could be a lot of fun."

Izzie stopped abruptly, drew a circle in the sand with the toe of her boot, and then sat down on a flat granite rock. "You fellas are all the same," she said. "Guns, guns, guns! I'd like to be a military messenger for the underground forces in France—lurking bravely behind enemy lines, delivering secret coded documents, hiding the notes in my school bag between the pages of my arithmetic book." She grinned. "I just know I could do it! I wouldn't be scared or anything. If someone stopped me, I'd just say, 'I'm Izzie Publicover on my way to school.' And they'd let me go through."

Jasper snorted. "Would you be saying it in German or in French? People might find it kind of funny that you were taking a shortcut through a field in France to get to your school in Granite Cove, Nova Scotia."

Izzie looked at Jasper and grinned. "Good old Jasper!" she said. "Always ready to take the wind out of my sails!"

Jasper smiled to himself and stared at the horizon. "Sorry," he said, "but you'd be a terrible spy. With hair that red and that frizzled with curls, you'd light up the whole countryside like a torch."

Izzie thought for a few moments. "Or I could be a military nurse," she said, "with a navy blue cape. I'd work in a big tent hospital, with bombs falling all around. I'd mop the perspiration off the foreheads of brave and handsome men, and hold their hands in mine when they were in pain from their wounds."

"Girls!" said Jasper. "They think nursing is all about mopping brows and holding hands. They never mention people throwing up or needing bedpans."

"Sometimes," said Izzie, as she got up to head for home, "I wish my best friend was a girl instead of a boy. Girls aren't so eager to step on your dreams and squash them into the ground."

CHAPTER N.º 2

By the time Izzie and Jasper reached their village, darkness was coming on, and it was almost time for supper.

"Thursday," said Izzie. "Macaroni and cheese. My favourite."

"And tomorrow's Friday. Fish. *My* favourite. Bye. See you tomorrow."

In the house, Izzie stomped the snow off her boots, hung up her coat and scarf, and put on her slippers. She suddenly realized that she was very hungry, as she opened the door into the kitchen. The macaroni and cheese smelled wonderful.

Her mother was sitting at the kitchen table, with her hands in her lap. Her father was lying on the couch beside the big black wood stove, reading *The Halifax Chronicle*. Joey, her seven-year-old brother, was on his stomach on the floor, reading comic books.

"Hey, Mum!" Izzie rushed over to give her mother a big hug. "Guess what? Jasper's going to be a fighter pilot and I'm going to be a spy. In six and a half years."

Her mum looked at Izzie, her face bleak. She was slumped down in the straight chair as though she was exhausted. "Six and a half years," she said, her voice thin and tired. "That long? Will the war last that long?" She looked as though ... *No,* thought Izzie, *it couldn't be*. But her mother did look as though she'd been crying.

Apparently, Mr. Publicover wasn't really reading. He was watching everything over the top of *The Chronicle*. Finally, he put it down and looked for a while at the ceiling—the soot marks, the cracks in the plaster. Then he sat up with his legs over the side of the couch, his hands clasped between his knees. His straight sand-coloured hair was lying on his head every which way, as though he'd been running his fingers through it.

"Maybe we should tell them," he said. "Why wait till after supper?"

Mrs. Publicover delivered a crooked smile. "Because," she said, "if we wait till then, maybe you'll all be able to eat something." Then she frowned. "But *I* certainly won't," she added in a low voice.

"Mum!" cried Izzie, with that familiar full-moon feeling grabbing the pit of her stomach. "What's all this *about?* Why do you look so *awful?* What's Dad *talking* about?" She grabbed her mother's arm so tightly that her fingers left red spots. But Mrs. Publicover didn't even seem to notice.

Izzie looked over at Joey. She raised her eyebrows in a question, but he shook his head and shrugged his shoulders. From the window,

Izzie could see the huge orange moon rising above the horizon. She glanced quickly at the calendar—the new one for 1942, with a picture of the king talking to some soldiers—and saw the round circle above today's date. So the moon hadn't been quite full last night after all. It was full tonight. That was why everyone was acting so weird, so *crazy*.

"*You* tell them, Jeff," said her mother to her dad. "I'm not up to it."

Mr. Publicover cleared his throat. "Kids," he began. "You know how mad I was when I tried to join the navy and they turned me down. Said they couldn't take me because I was too old—at *thirty-seven*—and also because ... well, because ... I had a family to look after."

"Which you still do," said his wife, looking hard at the kitchen floor. Was it Izzie's imagination, or did she look angry as well as sad? It was hard to tell.

"Well," continued her father, clearing his throat again, "I tried again last week. This afternoon I got word that they'd accepted me." He sat up straighter. "I'll be a sailor. I'll be good at my job. There's nothing about the sea that a fisherman doesn't know." He laughed. "Before too long, the admiral will be begging for my advice." He looked happy.

So did Joey. "My own dad!" he almost shouted. "In the navy! Just like Jimmy Conrad's father! You'll have a *uniform*! I can hardly wait to tell the kids in grade one!"

"All two of them," muttered Izzie, only half realizing that she'd said it. Her mind was criss-crossing over a lot of thoughts. *I guess I'm proud of him. Sure, I'm proud. But he'll be gone, maybe for a long time. He might get killed. Or he might get wounds so awful that I don't even want to think about them.*

But then she discovered she couldn't *stop* thinking about them. *Blindness. Leg wounds. How can you be a fisherman with only one leg? Or no hands? STOP, IZZIE!* Izzie squeezed her eyes shut and tried to make her mind into an empty cave.

It wasn't working. Izzie opened her eyes and looked at everyone. Joey was up on her father's lap, hugging him. Her dad was smiling. Her mother was finally up off her chair, spooning macaroni and cheese onto four plates. You couldn't say that she exactly *slammed* the plates onto the table, but you certainly heard them hit the surface, right through the blue-and-white checked tablecloth. Outside the window, the moon was well above the horizon, no longer orange, no longer warm. A cold moon, thought Izzie, as she sat down at the table, all her appetite gone.

CHAPTER *No.* 3

Izzie lay on her bed, watching the light from the white moon flickering on the ceiling. Because the moon was shining through a big dogwood tree on the front lawn and because it was a windy night, the ceiling looked alive with brightness and shadows. Izzie sighed. She'd probably done all the wrong things at suppertime when her father had delivered his news. To begin with, she hadn't eaten even one forkful of macaroni and cheese. And she was sure she hadn't smiled. Underneath the tablecloth, she had held her mother's hand, and that was probably bad, too. It would look as though she was taking sides—which, of course, she was. And taking sides in a matter that had already been decided wasn't really fair. After all, if you enlisted in the navy, you couldn't just turn around and change your mind.

Then she remembered trying not to look at anybody. She had just let her eyes dart around the kitchen, fixing themselves on items she seldom noticed—the big black wood stove and its lid-lifter's spiral handle; the old wooden clock that had belonged to her great-grandmother; the sampler that her godmother had given her, with the alphabet done in cross-stitch around the border and a message that said, "May your days be fruitful and number many"; the couch with its rumpled afghan; the flickering oil lamps; the pattern on the floor's linoleum.

Then, her father had said—so suddenly that she wasn't expecting it and had no time to think about her reply, "Well, Izzie, how do you feel about all this?"

Izzie had said the first thing that came into her head, her eyes still fixed on the linoleum, avoiding the hopeful, happy look on her dad's face.

"I don't want you to go! I hate it that you're going! I don't see why you want so badly to leave us and go out there on one of those big ships and get killed."

Then she'd leapt up and raced upstairs. When she reached the landing, she stopped for a moment and listened. A terrible silence reached her from the kitchen. She went into her room and slammed the door.

Now she lay on her bed and thought of all the things she should have done. Izzie frowned at the ceiling. *I could at least have said, "Congratulations," or "Good for you," or something nice.* When someone was mean to her friend Jasper, or when some other awful thing happened to him, he often said, "I feel like I've been smacked in the belly with a wet fish." Well, she'd just smacked her father in the belly with a wet fish. Maybe she should go down and say she was sorry. But she wasn't. Why *did* he want to go off and leave them? And saying you're sorry is such a hard thing to do. It's like saying, "I was wrong," and who wants to say *that?*

Izzie could hear Joey come up to bed and close his door. From downstairs, through the heat register, came the clatter of dishes and the murmur of voices. She shut her eyes and thought, *I didn't even dry the dishes, and it's supposed to be my job. Apparently, I'm not even on Mum's side.* Izzie turned over and buried her face in her pillow. But as she did, she heard the voices in the kitchen more clearly. She listened, barely breathing.

Mrs. Publicover's voice was sharper than usual and very easy to hear.

"But, Jeff," she said, "what'll we do with you gone? I know you'll get paid, but it may take a while for the money to reach us. It's not like we have a big fat bank account. The last time I looked, it had $23.64 in it. With gas and food rationed, our shop barely brings in enough money to cover our supplies. And we support your parents. That's six people."

Izzie's father's voice was lower, and Izzie had to hang her head over the side of her bed to hear. It wasn't as if she'd never done this before. She'd learned an awful lot about life and her parents by listening to what came up through that register.

"Your dad can tide you over till you get a job," her father was saying.

"A job?" Mrs. Publicover's voice was rising. "Where on earth in Granite Cove can I get a job? You might at least have warned me about all this, Jeff, instead of just coming up from the mailbox and dumping the whole awful mess in my lap. Have you thought about how I'll take care of the cows and all those chickens? Or shovel us out in winter?"

There was a short silence. Then Izzie heard her father say, "You've known for over a year that I wanted to join the navy. Did you expect me to stop trying after they turned me down the first time? You must have known it would happen sometime." His voice was getting louder, too.

For a few moments, Izzie sat up and stuck her

fingers in her ears. She hated it when her parents had fights like this. Or *discussions,* as her mother tried to call them. But she returned to her listening position quickly. She didn't want to miss anything.

The first words Izzie heard were, "... Dartmouth or Halifax or maybe Bridgewater. There's the rope works in Dartmouth, and the sugar refinery and the oil refinery. There's the shipyards in Halifax. Maybe there's something a woman can do there."

"Working at *what?*" Izzie's mother was starting to sound pretty frantic. "*You* may have married late, but *I* didn't. I'm only thirty. I had Izzie when I was nineteen, and there's not a single thing I know how to do except cook and do laundry and keep house."

"You could work as a maid in some fancy house," said her father.

"And just who," said her mother, "is going to want someone as a maid who is trailing two kids behind her?" She sniffed a couple of times and said, in a quavery voice, "And I don't want to live in someone's fancy house."

Then there was a long pause. Izzie guessed that her parents were making peace with each other and doing some kissing and hugging. That was good. Izzie needed some time for thinking about what she had just heard.

Moving away from Granite Cove! Whatever else Izzie was hearing, it was pretty clear that they were going to have to leave their house and go to some big city where her mother could get a job. She wouldn't be seeing Jasper every day—probably almost *never*—and she'd be going to another school. Probably a big school, with a bunch of kids in every grade—in their own class-rooms, instead of all in one room like in Granite Cove.

Then Izzie heard her father speak again. "You and I will go up to Halifax and Dartmouth tomorrow and look around. We'll look for a job for you, and we'll look for a place to live. I don't have to report for duty for nine days. It'll be OK. You'll see. I'll have you all set up and moved before I have to leave."

Izzie's mother gave a big gulp that came right up through the register. "I feel like it's the end of the world," she said.

Mr. Publicover sounded firm but kind. "Well," he said, "it's not. Think about it. They say that living in a big city can be wonderful. You may never want to come back here when the war's over. You'll wonder why you ever liked living in a fishing village."

When Izzie finally got to sleep that night, she had a lot of dreams, and they weren't all nightmares. She dreamed about the crowded Halifax streets, which she'd seen so recently with Joey and her father. In one dream they were in line to get into the Capitol Theatre, and they were almost at the door. In another, she was standing on Citadel Hill, watching a convoy sail out to sea. She saw her father waving from the deck of one of the ships. She waved back and felt very proud. When she woke up, she knew one thing she had to do before her parents left for the city that day.

Later in the morning, when her parents were getting ready to leave the house, Izzie stood up very straight in front of her father and said, "I have a speech to make."

He took off his cap and sat down on the nearest chair. "Fire away," he said.

Izzie cleared her throat and took a deep breath. "I'm sorry I said all those mad things to you last night," she said. "I know why this stupid war seems to be necessary. We sure don't want Hitler to jump across the Atlantic Ocean and just *take Canada*. We don't want him to put the whole

Publicover family in a concentration camp because we tell him he shouldn't be stealing countries or killing Jews. I think I know that this is a war that has to happen. I still hate it, but Mum told me once that you can't blame yourself for what you feel."

It was time for Izzie to take another deep breath. Her father just sat there, waiting.

Izzie went on talking. "So I know they have to have people to fight the war. Dad—I had a dream last night. I was standing on Citadel Hill, and a convoy was going by. I could see your ship, and there you were in your new sailor suit, waving to us. And Dad?" Izzie paused in her speech.

"Yes?" he said. "What?"

"I just wanted you to know that I felt so proud of you." One big wet tear squeezed out of her eye and rolled down her cheek. "And that's the end of my speech."

Izzie's father got up from his chair and wrapped both his arms around her in a big hug. They stayed like that for quite a while. In the meantime, Mrs. Publicover was blowing her nose and cleaning off her glasses, while Joey just stood there, looking confused.

Then they all left the house—Izzie and Joey to school, and their parents off to Halifax and Dartmouth. Joey shot up the hill past Mr. Henkel's bark pots and the Knickles' barn, eager to tell his two best friends that in nine days, his father was going to be a *sailor*. He felt proud enough to burst his coat buttons.

Izzie watched until her father filled up his tank with gasoline from the pump outside their house and shop. She saw the red liquid in the big cylinder go down—slowly, slowly—and then she saw it splash up until it was full again. Usually, she loved seeing that happen, but today, her eyes and her mind were half closed. Then she saw the truck bump over the potholes in the road and disappear around Mr. Jollimore's hill.

She took her time on her way to school, clumping through the snow in her big boots, kicking at chunks of ice, not caring if she was

*He wrapped both his arms
around her in a big hug.
They stayed like that
for quite a while.*

late. What did it matter? Before very long, she wouldn't even be going to that school. Almost without realizing she was doing it, Izzie walked all the way around the Henkels' bark pots and retraced her steps. She could feel a big lump rising in her throat. If she was going to howl like a baby, she'd better do it in her own kitchen. She didn't want a bunch of kids staring at her while she spilled tears all over her desk.

Mr. and Mrs. Publicover weren't expected to return until eight o'clock that evening. Izzie had made supper for herself and Joey at five o'clock, out of two wieners, some sauerkraut, and two eggs. She knew that they were the last eggs in the cupboard, but she figured that the hens would provide some more by morning. She went out to the barn, milked the three cows, and shovelled out the manure. She left Joey inside to wash the dishes. That wasn't one of his jobs, but neither was shovelling manure one of hers.

As Izzie worked, she wondered who'd look after the cows and chickens when they were gone. Would someone live in their house, or would it be all closed up, like a tomb? Would they be able to take Adella with them when they moved? Adella was rubbing against her legs right now and purring.

Izzie felt very tired as she poured the buckets of milk into the tall tin containers. All her energy had been sucked out of her by sadness.

At eight o'clock, Joey and Izzie watched as their parents stamped the snow from their boots and hung up their outdoor clothes in the back porch. No one knew that Izzie had heard every-thing through the register the night before, and she wasn't about to tell anyone. If her parents realized the kinds of things she heard through that register, they might start having their private talks in the cold front parlour. So when her parents came in and sat down at the kitchen table, Izzie just said, "Well?"

"Well what?" said her mother, reaching for the hot cup of tea that Izzie was pouring out for her. The Publicovers always kept the teapot sitting on the back of the stove, adding tea and water throughout the day. By now, it was almost black. "Wonderful!" said Mrs. Publicover, warming her cold hands on the thick mug.

"Well—what did you do in the city?" said Izzie, looking at them very hard.

Mr. Publicover was smiling with his mouth and frowning with his eyebrows. "Izzie," he said. "Joey. We have a lot of things to tell you."

Izzie sat down on the big rocking chair. This wasn't going to be a good time to be standing up. She wanted something strong underneath her.

"OK," she said, her voice a little bit rough. "Then tell us."

CHAPTER N° 5

It was their father who told them what they were waiting to hear. Their parents had been busy during that long day in the city. After they arrived in Halifax, they drove right through to the ferry wharf. They'd heard that rents in Dartmouth were cheaper than in Halifax, so they decided to look for a job for Mrs. Publicover over there. They drove their truck onto the ferry, paid their thirty cents, and walked up to the upper deck. From there they could see all the Canadian and foreign ships tied up at the docks or moving into Bedford Basin.

They found a job for Mrs. Publicover surprisingly quickly. So many of the workers at the Acadia Sugar Refinery had gone off to war that there were openings on the assembly line.

"What's that?" Izzie asked.

Her mother half-frowned and said, "I'm not quite sure. A bunch of people are in a lineup, I think, at some sort of counter. Something on the counter—a belt, I think it's called—is moving, and as articles come by on the belt, each person in the line has to do something like close a bag, or stick a label onto it, or stamp it with a number. That kind of thing."

"All day?" asked Izzie. "Just stamp, stamp, stamp, or close, close, close? *All day long?*"

"Sounds boring," said Joey.

Mr. Publicover was looking uncomfortable. But his wife smiled. "It's OK. I don't have to be able to type or take shorthand or know anything at all. That's what frightened me. Now I don't need to be scared to death of acting dumb. The man in charge said the job was so easy that a child of seven could do it."

"Me!" said Joey. "Just like me."

"And we found a place to live, too," said their mother.

Now it was Izzie's turn to be afraid. She didn't want to live anywhere but in her own house.

"A woman who works in the office lives in one of the company houses owned by the refinery. There's a long row of them. Her husband is … somewhere else … so the house is almost empty. She says we can have two rooms on the second floor and share the kitchen and bathroom."

"Two rooms?" said Izzie. "Just two little rooms?"

"They're not all that little," her mother said. "And Izzie …"

"What?"

"Did you hear me? I said *bathroom*. She has a toilet that flushes, and when you turn on the tap at the sink, hot water comes out. Imagine!"

Izzie thought about that.

"And the school? Is it miles away? Are there a million kids in it? And what about Adella?" Izzie had picked up the cat and was hugging her. "Can she come with us, too, and live in our *two rooms?*" Izzie felt as stiff and frozen as an icicle.

Her mother actually *laughed*. "It's going to be OK," she said. "Mrs. Ross—Rosalie Ross, that's her name—loves cats, but her husband was allergic to them. Now he's ... not there ... so she's dying to have Adella in the house. And listen—"

"What?" said Joey.

"Electric lights! Push a switch, and they come on! We can get a little radio and plug it in. Rosalie even has a *washing machine* in the basement. It has a wringer thing that you can send the clothes through, and it squeezes out the water. I've lived in Granite Cove all my life, so I never even *saw* one before. Not a real one. Just pictures."

Izzie didn't care about the washing machine. "And the school?"

"Down the road a fair bit," said her mother. "But more kids. More friends."

But not Jasper. Izzie didn't say that out loud. She just thought it. But she guessed her mother must be reading her mind. She came over and put her arm around Izzie's shoulder.

"I know it'll be hard to leave Jasper," she said. "*Really hard.* We're all going to find it sad to leave our friends. But we'll meet new ones. And it's not forever. Just till the war's over. Maybe soon."

Joey didn't like that idea. "Not too soon. Not till I'm old enough to be a sailor like Dad."

Mrs. Publicover didn't respond to that remark. She just produced a thin smile and changed the subject.

"Your dad has to leave in one week. So we have to make the move while he's still around to help us. Tomorrow's Saturday. We can all work like oxen. We'll have to decide what to leave behind and what to take—clothes, toys, pictures, little things to remind us of home." Suddenly their mother started to look sad again. And Izzie was thinking, *This is happening too fast. It's not fair!*

Their father spoke quickly. "Your mum's very tired. So off you go upstairs and get ready for bed. Tomorrow will be a long day."

By that time, both Joey and Izzie had heard everything they needed or wanted to know. Joey couldn't figure out how he felt about moving to the city. Izzie knew exactly how she felt.

Later, Izzie listened through the register to her parents talking. She heard her mother say, "How did I do, Jeff? Did I sound like a big brave mother?"

He laughed. "You were great. Or, like they say about some movie stars, *sensational*. You should've been an actress. No one would've guessed what you really feel about those two rooms. Or about the assembly line."

"Well," said Izzie out loud to herself, as she crawled back under her covers, "*That* certainly doesn't make me feel any better."

CHAPTER N° 6

Saturday was miserable. That was the best word that Izzie could think of to describe it. That, and also *terrible, tiring, sad, confusing,* and—yes— *angry*. It was an angry day. She found that as she packed boxes and piled clothes into the family trunk, she was feeling full of fury. At whom? She stopped for a minute or two and thought about that. At Hitler, for making all this work and upheaval necessary. At her father, for being so brave and patriotic. At her mother, because she said Izzie could only take five of her books and two of her bears, and she couldn't understand

why Izzie wanted to take a dirty old Raggedy
Ann doll that she hadn't played with since she was
eight. ("She's a piece of home," Izzie had said,
hugging the doll for the first time in three years.)
She also felt mad at Jasper because he could go on
living in Granite Cove, and she couldn't.

When Izzie saw Jasper piling buoys on his
father's wharf, she threw on her outdoor clothes
and went down to join him. She didn't even say
hi. She said, "We're going away."

"I know," he said. "My dad said so. Your
father told him this morning when they both
went out to milk the cows. It made him some
jealous. My dad, I mean."

"Why jealous?" said Izzie. "That's just stupid."

"It's *not*. He wants to join the navy too, but he's
got those thick glasses, and they won't take him."

"Well," said Izzie, frowning, "it's still stupid.
When my dad comes home all shot to bits—or
doesn't come home *at all*—your father will still
be walking around, as healthy as a horse. He
won't be jealous *then*."

"Well, don't sound so mad. I don't want you to move away." Jasper stopped talking. Then he added. "But you're lucky. I wish I was you."

"I'm *not* lucky," snapped Izzie. "We have to go live in two tiny little rooms, and I can only take five books, and my dad's maybe going to get torpedoed, and we'll be living with a woman we don't even *know*. I *hate* all that."

Jasper frowned. "Maybe so, but it'll be a big adventure. You'll see the huge battleships up close and hear the air-raid sirens practising. And you'll have electric lights and even a radio. And when we're freezing to death in our outhouses in February, you'll be sitting in your nice warm bathroom. And you'll have a ton of new friends. Sure sounds lucky to me."

Izzie thought about how scared it made her just to *think* about that ton of new friends. "You're not even *trying* to understand, Jasper Morash," she said, turning around and stomping her way back to her own house.

Back home, it wasn't any better. Her mother

was in a weird mood—sometimes smiling and energetic, but often so silent and serious that she didn't even notice when her children spoke to her. Joey was cheerful—*too* cheerful—and almost totally useless at helping.

At noon, Mr. Publicover came home with some news that lit him up like a lantern.

"Hey, Bess!" he said to his wife, acting as if the kids weren't even there. "Guess what?! Great news! You know those Eisners who are gonna move here from Sambro? Well, Mr. Eisner wants to rent our house while they get their own place built. He'll keep the cows and hens and sell the milk and eggs. And also run the little shop. That'll give them enough to pay the rent, and we'll have some extra income for my mom and dad."

Mrs. Publicover looked stricken. "Does that mean that I'll have to clear out all the dressers and closets and pack all our stuff away in the attic?"

"Well ... yes."

Mrs. Publicover sighed. "I know I should be thrilled to death," she said, "because I *was* worried about the cows and the chickens and the shop. But ..."

"But what?"

"Knowing about the Eisners is just making me feel even more frantic." And that's exactly how she looked. "So much work," she muttered and closed her eyes.

Mr. Publicover walked over to the middle of the kitchen (with his outdoor boots on!) and gave her a big hug. "Never mind, Bessie," he said. "This, too, shall pass."

Izzie and her parents worked long and hard on Saturday and Sunday. Izzie did what she could to help after school during the following week. Even Joey made himself useful, carting things up and down the stairs and running errands.

Mrs. Morash came over to do some of the lifting and packing and scrubbing, and on the last day before they left—Friday—Jasper skipped school and was as good a worker as anyone else. Finally the house looked perfect—and very bare.

Then, just as they were all about to collapse in a heap on the floor—exhausted but pleased with the completion of their job—the old clock in the kitchen struck five.

At the moment when the fifth gong stopped ringing, the outside door opened. There wasn't even a knock. About twenty people yelled, "Surprise!" and came in through the back porch. Everyone was carrying something. Mrs. Henkel had brought her special coconut squares; Mrs. Hennessey had cooked two chickens—big ones; there were potato salads in bowls, tubs of sauerkraut, and mountains of homemade bread. Everyone had brought what they did or baked best—ignoring all the ration coupons they'd had to use in order to make this party perfect. There were also presents. A silver bracelet for

Mrs. Publicover. A navy blue wool sweater for Mr. Publicover. A beautiful little yellow dory that Mr. Knickle had made for Joey, with tiny oars and thole-pins. A brand new bear for Izzie— large, soft, and squishy. And right now, she badly needed something to hug.

It was a perfect goodbye party. Joe Murphy had brought his fiddle, and people step-danced and polkaed in the kitchen, in the parlour, and in the shop. They all sang special Maritime songs and drank a lot of homemade root beer. Mrs. Publicover tried not to think about the big mess that was being made of their spotless house.

But one of the best parts of the party was yet to come. At 8:30, Mrs. Morash announced that all the Publicovers, including Adella, had to sit down and not move. Then the women—and even some of the men—tidied up the house, cleaned the floor, and washed the dishes. When they all left—at 9:15—laughing, crying, singing— the place looked as tidy and as perfect as when they'd arrived.

About twenty people yelled, "Surprise!" and came in through the back porch.

Afterwards, Izzie went upstairs and cried into her pillow—quietly, so that no one would hear. Inside her head, she said, *That was just about the nicest and the saddest party that I ever went to.*

CHAPTER N⁰ 7

Izzie woke up early and peered out into the dark morning. She wouldn't be able to see much until about seven o'clock, but she didn't want to miss a single thing. This would be the last morning she'd be able to look at that scene she loved so well—for heaven only knew how long. By ten o'clock, the truck—already packed, with a huge tarpaulin covering their trunk and suitcases and boxes—would be on the road, headed for Halifax and Dartmouth. A whole new life was staring her in the face, and the next year was one big question mark. This was a scary feeling.

But there was a piece of her—quite a large chunk—that was starting to think some hopeful thoughts. For instance, what would it feel like to press a button or flick a switch and have a light come on? It was hard to imagine anything that easy. And no lamp chimneys to clean or cows to milk or water to haul out of the well. To have water come out of a tap—*both hot and cold*— would seem like some sort of a miracle to her. And she might find a best friend who was a *girl*. She *might*.

Then Izzie remembered another reason for getting up so early. She'd decided that she'd go out and milk all three cows this morning, instead of just one. She wanted to do something nice for her father, and this seemed as good a thing as any.

Out in the barn, Izzie stroked the back of her favourite cow—Clementine, the gentle one she always milked—and laid the side of her head against the cow's flank. When Clementine was a little calf, Izzie had named her. She'd read the name in a book of babies' names, and it meant "mild, calm, merciful." Suddenly she felt guilty for being so pleased about not having to milk Clementine every morning. She'd forgotten how much she loved her—those kind brown eyes, her warm breath, her large and comforting body. She could write letters to her dad and to Jasper. There was nothing at all she could do for Clementine. Izzie felt that familiar tightness in her throat and itching at the corners of her eyes.

No, she would *not* cry. As soon as she'd wakened up this morning, she'd vowed to act happy *all day*. She wasn't going to go galumphing around during the last two days before her father set out on his own new adventure. Imagine what she'd feel like if her father got wounded or drowned or some other gruesome thing, and she hadn't even tried to be nice during his last days at home. So she returned to the house with a stiff smile fixed onto her face.

By the time the Publicover truck left for Halifax and Dartmouth, the morning fog had cleared, and Granite Cove was as beautiful as Izzie had ever seen it. The sea was a brilliant blue beside the white rocks, hills, and fields, and the evergreen trees were laden with last night's snowfall.

All along the road around the edge of the cove, women and kids came out from their porches and decks to wave them goodbye, and down on the wharves and in the boats, men stood up from their work on nets and buoys and barrels, shouting out their farewells.

And there, standing against the Morash mailbox, was Jasper, holding a package in his hand. "It's a big box of notepaper," he said, as he handed the parcel up to Izzie. "Write me a lot of letters."

Izzie could just nod. She couldn't manage to speak.

"And don't forget us!" he yelled, as the truck moved on. Izzie shook her head hard and hoped no one saw the tear sliding down her cheek.

Then the truck turned the corner around Mr. Jollimore's hill, and the Cove was gone. They were in the deep woods now, on their way to the main road into Halifax.

Halifax wasn't all that far from Granite Cove, but it took a long time to get there. The snowplow had been through once, but the snow was heavy and the road slippery.

When they finally entered Halifax and were driving down Robie Street, the Noon Gun on the Citadel—which boomed forth every day at twelve o'clock—blasted out over the city. Hearing that cannon go off made Izzie half wonder if they'd driven to Halifax just in time to see the arrival of the Nazis on the shores of Halifax Harbour.

But it was OK. When they drove along Water Street to the ferry dock, the harbour seemed as calm and peaceful as Granite Cove. And on the ferry they could see way up toward Bedford Basin, where many ships lay at anchor, waiting for the next convoy to leave. From the other side of the ferry, they looked far beyond the battle-ships and tugs to the harbour mouth and the wide horizon. Izzie watched all this from the top deck of the ferry. Maybe living in the city wouldn't be so bad after all. This was pretty interesting.

She remembered for a moment about the huge explosion that had destroyed a third of Halifax in 1917, when a Belgian ship had collided with a vessel from France called the *Mont Blanc,* which was carrying many tons of ammunition. She knew that almost two thousand people had been killed and thousands wounded. Many had been blinded by flying glass.

But Izzie swept these thoughts out of her mind. That would never happen a second time. They'd be extra careful now about keeping ships from crashing into one another. They might have been dumb about that in 1917. In 1942 they'd be too smart to let a thing like that ever occur again. Besides, it would be like lightning striking the same place twice. No. It would just never, never take place during this war.

When the Publicover truck drove off the ferry into Dartmouth, the family didn't have far to go. They were on their way to Woodside, on the outskirts of the town—to the sugar refinery, the assembly line, the new school, the house with their two rooms, a whole new life. Izzie could feel a knot in her stomach tighten as they drove farther down the shore to their destination.

CHAPTER N°. 8

January 22, 1942

Dear Jasper,

Thank you for all that notepaper. There's so much of it that you must think I'm going to be away for twenty years.

Here's a letter. It's Saturday—a week since we left—and I don't have a new best friend yet. So I have the whole day to write this. I'll make it long, long, long, so you won't think you wasted your money on all that paper.

On the way here we had a ferry ride. You'd like that. Lots of big ships. You can't believe how many. Then we got off and drove to our new home. That sounds real weird. <u>New home</u>.

When we knocked on the door, this lady opened it. Just wait till you meet her. She's wild looking, with great big earrings and bunches and bushels of blond hair (<u>very</u> blond. Like yellow). It's as curly as mine only much longer. She wears tight skirts and red blouses and high heels. Also, a ton of lipstick and smelly face powder. I never met anyone like her. If she came to Granite Cove, people wouldn't know what to say or do.

But she gave us a big welcome. She hugged Mum and me and Joey, and she shook hands with Dad. Then she helped us in with all our ten tons of stuff.

The two rooms aren't so awful. They're not all that small. Joey and I have to sleep in one room. Too bad. He snores, and he's also nosy about my belongings. Pokes around and <u>investigates</u> things. So I'm not going to write a diary. I'll write you instead.

Pause. *Time out for lunch. Peanut butter sandwich
and an apple. Mum only has one hour off at noon.
That's not long enough to cook a meal. So we eat
dinner at night.*

Afternoon. *The wild-looking lady's name is Rosalie
Ross. She looks like a Rosalie. She's divorced. I've
never ever known anyone who was divorced. She works
at Mum's sugar refinery in the office. I asked Mum
what Rosalie's work is. She says she "does the books."
Those are her very words. That means she does a lot
of things about money. Mum told us that everyone
says that even though she looks like a floozy (whatever
that means), she's the smartest person in the office.*

*I don't care if Rosalie is smart or dumb. We all
love her. She buys special cat food for Adella and
sings when she's cooking. She says that having us
here makes her house come alive. She told us she
always wanted kids but never got any. She whispered
to me last week when we were alone in the kitchen
doing the dishes that she had a baby once, but it was
born too soon and died. It only weighed two pounds.
So she really loves having us in the house. She said*

that if she had a red-haired husband, she could have a daughter who looked exactly like me—frizzly hair and all.

Dad left on Sunday. We don't know where he is, because he's not allowed to tell. We saw one convoy go out, but (unlike in my dream) the ships were too far away to see the men on them. I wonder if he's in the middle of the ocean. I'm so scared he'll get torpedoed. I hate it that he's not here. Mum looks very <u>serious</u> most of the time. What's she thinking? She's acting sort of <u>vacant</u> right now—like she's all alone inside her head. I try not to ask her too many questions.

I'm glad Rosalie is here, with her shining red blouses and necklaces and bracelets. This is a sad time, so I like it that she sings while she's working. She and Mum take turns getting dinner.

I'm stopping here for a cookie and milk.

School is almost a mile away. There are fifty kids in my room. There's a girl who watches me, so maybe she wants to be my friend. Her name is Roberta. I'm too shy to say hello. I've never been shy in my entire life before, but being in one room with fifty strangers takes all the starch out of me.

On Thursday, a new kid came to our class. Her name is Patricia. Not Patsy or Pat. She's from England. The teacher calls her a "guest child." Her parents sent her over here to rescue her from the bombs that are falling on London. Poor sad parents! Wouldn't that be terrible? She must feel like she's been tossed away. I have a feeling that she's even more scared than I am, but she stands up very straight, as though she's used to being brave.

I'm going to stop soon. My hand is tired and so are my eyes.

I wish you lived here. And I miss the fishing boats and having my own room. But this is OK. Rosalie says we can use the whole house, because she's away so much. She works all day on weekdays. At night she often goes to the movies or dancing with sailors or soldiers. On weekends she usually goes to see her sick mother in Truro.

Three more things. Listen to this: A bathroom with a white toilet that flushes. Hot water out of the tap if you turn on a oil heater. And electric lights. Flick the switch and up comes the light. You can read at night without wrecking your eyes.

> *Yours sincerely,*
> *Your friend,*
> *Izzie*

Rosalie's house was on a flat piece of land behind the sugar refinery. You couldn't see the harbour from there, but if you crossed the road and field and stood on the edge of the hill, above where the Big Houses were—where the important executives lived—you had a wide and beautiful view of the harbour.

Not far off was one end of the huge gate that closed the entrance to Halifax Harbour to any dangerous ships or submarines that might manage to sneak into the inner waters to do what Izzie thought of as "terrible deeds." Terrible deeds were shooting people and blowing up ships and destroying the city. To Izzie all of this seemed frightening, as well as sort of exciting. As the days passed, she often crossed the road and stood on the hill above the harbour—watching convoys arriving and leaving, looking at the weird zigzag patterns that were camouflaging the ships, listening to the air-raid sirens practising, making up stories about make-believe battles.

By now—mid-February—Izzie had two almost-best friends. One was Roberta—who lived in one of the Big Houses close to the water. The other was Patricia, the English "guest child."

Roberta seemed to like Izzie a lot—but not for any reason that Izzie could figure out. Later on, Roberta would tell her that she'd wanted to be her friend because of Izzie's crazy curly red hair and her million freckles—and because of the way Izzie had of saying what she felt like saying, and doing what she felt like doing, without worrying about what other people thought. By the end of Izzie's second week in Woodside, she'd stopped being shy and scared. She'd started being exactly who she'd always been. But Roberta had always been shy, and it didn't look as though she was ever going to change. It was as though she *needed* Izzie.

Izzie's friendship with Patricia was different. Patricia seemed to be comfortable with her, and Izzie thought she knew why. Both she and Patricia were unlike all the other students. Their clothes were different, for one thing. Apparently, kids who lived in a fishing village or in England wore skirts and sweaters and coats that didn't look one bit like the ones that the Woodside kids had on. Mrs. Publicover sewed or knitted most of her clothes, and Izzie guessed that in England, even store-bought clothes weren't like Canadian ones.

Also, Patricia and Izzie didn't speak the same way as the other kids did. Some of the grade sixes tried to make fun of their accents, but the teacher—Miss Miller—heard them doing it and landed on them like a ton of cement. She even sent stern letters to their parents, saying that their children would be sent home if they were heard teasing Patricia or Izzie even *once*. So all that mean stuff stopped. But if you sound different from everyone else, you know it, even if people don't talk about it anymore.

In any case, Patricia started tagging along with Roberta and Izzie, everywhere they went. And more and more, she did a lot of talking.

"Why is your hair so curly?" she asked Izzie.

"Because I was born that way."

"And yours?" She looked at Roberta.

"It's really dead straight," said Roberta. "I have a permanent wave. They put your hair in rollers, hook hot clips over the rollers, and then— *presto*—you have curly hair!"

Patricia wrinkled up her nose. "Mother says that it's ridiculous to give permanent waves to children," she said. She had short brown hair, as straight as a pencil, held off her forehead with a bobby pin.

Later that day Patricia said, "You don't have much of a war here."

Later that day Patricia said,
"You don't have much
of a war here."

Izzie could feel a lump of anger rise in her chest. "We do so," she said. "Look at all those ships. There's a gate over there to keep submarines out of the harbour. My dad is in the navy. He might get killed any minute. Haven't you heard the air-raid sirens practising? Don't you have blackout curtains in Mrs. Whatshername's house where you live?"

Patricia was walking so straight that she looked as though she'd swallowed a mop handle. "Her name's Mrs. Johnstone. Yes, of course she has blackout curtains. Everyone in the *world* has blackout curtains. And *my* father's in the navy, too. He's a *commander.* What's yours?"

"What's mine? I don't get it."

"What's his rank? A lieutenant? A captain? A *what*?"

Izzie frowned. Then she laughed. "Well," she said, "he's not an admiral. He's a sailor in a sailor suit."

"Oh!" said Patricia, looking straight down her sharp nose. "A *rating.*"

"I don't care what he is," snapped Izzie. "He's a brave man. Also handsome. And I bet he knows more about the sea than your dad does. He used to be a fisherman."

"A *fisherman!*"

"Yes." Izzie was feeling wilted, but she wasn't going to let Patricia know that. "So—what's your dad do when he's not being a commander?"

"He's ... sort of a lawyer." Patricia looked at her feet for a moment as she walked along. Then she said again, "No. Not much of a war here."

Roberta sighed. "OK," she said. "Tell us about *your* war."

Patricia perked up. "Bombs. Houses falling down. Collapsing like a pack of cards. Or whole walls falling off like a doll's house. Air-raid sirens that *mean* something. Not just practising for something that'll never happen. Same with your stupid searchlights. *Our* searchlights find *planes*. And then we shoot them down. This is just a sissy war over here."

Izzie looked at Roberta, and they both rolled their eyes. But Izzie felt a little itch of envy in the back of her neck. She wished she'd seen things that were that dangerous, that terrifying, that *exciting*. She couldn't stop herself from asking, "Weren't you scared?"

"Scared?" Patricia gave a little scornful snort. "In my family, we're not even allowed to *talk* about being scared. My mother never even blinked an eye when a bomb hit the house next door to us. It was just like a pile of grey powder when we went to look at it—after the all-clear sounded."

"And the people?" You could hardly hear Roberta's voice.

"More grey powder. You don't really think anyone would walk out from under all that devastation, do you?"

"Did you *know* those people?" Izzie almost hated to ask.

"Of course," said Patricia, standing up a little straighter.

There was a long, long silence.

Then Patricia spoke again. Her voice sounded different to Izzie, but she wasn't sure it really was. "I'm ashamed to admit it," said Patricia, "but I started to cry that day. But mother became very angry and made me stop. We're not supposed to cry in our house—not ever."

"Not even if you're hurt, like if you break an arm or something? Or if someone *dies?*" Izzie frowned.

"No."

"Never?"

"No," said Patricia. "Not even when your parents send you all the way across the Atlantic Ocean to live with a lot of total strangers." Then she said, "Let's go home. I'm hungry."

They all went to their separate houses. No one said another word.

CHAPTER N° 10

March 7

Dear Dad,

I don't know where you are, but I bet some navy postman will be able to find you. Mum says the navy is very smart about finding people.

I hope you like being a sailor as much as you thought you would. It seems to me it must be pretty cold out there, smack in the middle of the Atlantic Ocean. Remember the calendar that we had in our kitchen last year? In case you forget, it was a corvette,

*tossing around in a lot of huge waves and <u>covered
with ice</u>. I think of you as being on one of those
ships. Please don't slip on all that ice and fall
overboard.*

Your loving daughter,
Izzie

*P.S. I'll write a bunch of letters and send them
in the same envelope. This will make a big fat
package, and maybe then it won't get lost or fall
behind some navy radiator or slither overboard on
the ice.*

xo Izzie

March 10

Dear Dad,

*I told you before about Roberta. She's one of my
best friends now but very quiet and shy. She lives
in the assistant manager's house down by the water.
It's really big, with a shiny dining-room table, and
chairs in the living room with padded cretonne seats*

*and backs. Cretonne is a kind of flowered cloth. I
love to look at them, but I'm scared to sit on them.
Roberta says she's only allowed to sit on them
when she's clean, and I'm almost never clean.
That's because I play softball a lot and kick-the-can,
and sit on fences, and sometimes wash the truck for
Mum.*

*I like school. I thought I'd be in a room with kids
who were all in my grade. I'm not. There are about
fifty kids in our room, and they're in three grades.
So I can still listen to what's going on in the other
grades. I love doing that.*

*Patricia often acts like she's the Queen of the
Castle, but I like her—partly because she's sort of
mysterious. It's almost like she has a secret she's
not telling. Mum says she "blows hot and cold."
That means that sometimes she behaves like
royalty, and other times she folds all up inside
herself and seems almost frightened—but never
says so. When I'm scared, I say so. Then the fear
often goes somewhere else and leaves me alone.
Not Patricia. No complaining, no crying, no*

yelling, not even big sighs. If she's feeling any sad
things, they must all be squeezed up tight and
stuffed down inside her.

Don't fall in. If anyone shoots, duck.

Love xo
Izzie

March 15

Dear Dad,

I love Rosalie, but she's almost never around.
When she is, she lights up the house and makes us
all happy with her dancing and singing while she
does the dusting or cuts up the vegetables for dinner.
I certainly don't dance while I dust. I just go at it
real <u>fast</u> so that it'll be <u>over</u> and <u>done</u>.

Rosalie has a lot of boyfriends. She says she's
"playing the field" and that she doesn't want to get
married again. "Once," she said yesterday, "is enough."
Mum says Rosalie attracts men like flies. I love to
watch her get all dressed up to go out. She has lots of

dangly earrings—some like pretend diamonds. She calls them <u>rhinestones</u>. Her dresses always seem to be black or red, and when she finishes putting all the stuff on her face, she looks like a gypsy or a movie star. I hope when I grow up I'll attract men like flies, because she seems to have a lot of fun. If that's going to happen, I'll have to figure out some way to get rid of my freckles.

Joey is fine. He has two best friends. Mum is OK, but I don't think she's madly in love with the assembly line. We all miss you.

Love,
Izzie

P.S. Rosalie gave me a pair of her earrings. Each one has a bright red stone, with tiny miniature chains that dribble down from it. (When no one's around, I put them on and smile at myself in the mirror. They look great with my wild red hair.)

xo Izzie

While Izzie was folding up the letters to put them in a big envelope, she thought about her father and about the old days when they were all together. Then something happened that really worried her. A shiver shot right up her spine. *She suddenly realized that she couldn't remember what her father looked like.* And there weren't any pictures of him in this house—not even one.

Izzie put down her pen and went over to the window, being careful to turn off the light before she pulled aside the blackout curtain. It was a dark night, and even the stars were very dim. Up in the sky, searchlights were weaving back and forth, back and forth, criss-crossing each other, moving slowly, carefully. Overhead, she could hear a plane, and suddenly one of the lights caught it in its beam. The light followed it as it moved across the sky, and Izzie remembered Patricia talking about shooting the planes down in England. But that wasn't going to happen here. They were just practising. Izzie sighed. Perhaps Patricia was right. Maybe it wasn't much of a war here. Izzie wished that something a little bit exciting would happen.

She felt guilty about having such a terrible wish, but for the hundredth time, she remembered her mother saying that you couldn't help what you felt.

CHAPTER N° 11

Izzie looked at the calendar in her room.
It was April 9, which meant that almost three months had gone by since she'd even *seen* Granite Cove, or Jasper, or the little orange schoolhouse, or the fishing boats bringing in their lobsters. She liked living in Woodside, and she enjoyed the big wide world that had opened up for her—with its electric lights, the radio, the harbour full of ships, new friends, bathrooms, and, once in a while, even a *movie.* But today she felt homesick. She longed to press her head against Clementine's warm side and hug her

neck. Was there anything in the world as comforting as your own *cow?*

"And just look at that soggy old world out there!" Izzie actually said it out loud. It was April, and wasn't March 21 supposed to be the first day of spring? Izzie was sick of hearing Patricia talk about spring in England.

"I detest your climate," she had said yesterday. Izzie could feel herself gritting her teeth. "At *home* we get daffodils in February. And in April, it's gorgeous."

Izzie had looked at the damp muddy ground and at the snow that was still lingering in low places and around the roots of trees. She couldn't think of a thing to say.

But this was another day, and maybe something good would happen.

In school, Miss Miller started their English class with a quote from a poem by Robert Browning. "This poem is for Patricia," she said, and started to read. Izzie would always remember the first two lines:

Oh to be in England
Now that April's there

She looked over at Patricia. She was staring at the top of her desk, and there was no expression on her face. But she was holding onto her pencil case so tightly that her knuckles were white. Izzie wanted to go over, put her hand on her shoulder, and say, "Go on, Patricia. Have a good cry."

But of course she didn't.

However, later on Izzie did ask Patricia if she wanted to come over for dinner that night. It was Rosalie's turn to cook, and she never minded if extra people turned up. Patricia had once said that she thought Rosalie was *vulgar*. "All that fake jewellery," she said, "those tight skirts, those patent leather pumps. I'd die if my mother looked like that."

Well, Izzie didn't want her own mother to look exactly like that either, but she hoped that Rosalie would go on looking like that for as long as she lived. She didn't want her ever to change.

Maybe if Patricia saw Rosalie in her own kitchen, humming and singing and being so *happy,* she'd feel differently about her. It was recess time when Izzie asked her.

"Yes, please," said Patricia, as polite and prim as a grown woman. "I'd like that ever so much. Particularly this evening. It's been a perfectly horrid afternoon." This was one of her royalty days.

That evening, Rosalie cooked dinner for Izzie and Joey and their mother—and for Patricia. Patricia sat on one of the straight-backed kitchen chairs and watched everything—Rosalie dancing across the kitchen from counter to stove, Izzie setting the table, Mrs. Publicover measuring out the coffee, Joey reading the comics in *The Halifax Chronicle.*

You couldn't tell what she was thinking by looking at her face, but she never once—all evening long—mentioned British warfare or her father's high rank or the Canadian climate.

There were a few tense minutes when Rosalie sang both verses of "The White Cliffs of Dover" while she was whipping the cream for the gingerbread. Patricia's knuckles got white again, and she said, through lips that scarcely moved, "We *never* get whipped cream in England. Over *there,* whipping cream is for our brave soldiers."

Rosalie replied, as bright as a button, "Well, we don't have much here, either, because it gets used on the ships going to England. But having you to dinner makes this a special occasion, so we're just going to pull out all the stops and *have* it. Same with the gingerbread. Lots of ration coupons— but who cares?" Then she clicked across the kitchen in her high heels and popped the gingerbread into the oven.

After dinner, Izzie and Patricia washed the dishes, and Joey set the table for breakfast.

Then the three of them played Monopoly for a while before Patricia had to leave. Rosalie and Izzie walked Patricia home in the dark—just two doors down, in one of the other company houses.

"A successful party," said Rosalie on the way home. "She smiled four times. I counted."

"Four times is real good," said Izzie, shaking her head. "I'd give anything to know what's going on inside that head of hers. Maybe we'll never know. But she's a puzzle I'm dying to solve."

They took the long way home, walking down to the hill behind Roberta's house. From there, they could see the outer harbour below them, shining faintly in the darkness. A large vessel stood at anchor, not far from shore, silhouetted against the water.

Izzie shivered. "It looks so dark and lonely and huge," she said, "as if no one was aboard."

Rosalie laughed. "Oh," she said, "there are plenty of men on board. I'm going to the movies

79

with one of them tomorrow night. She's called the *Trongate*. Nobody'd better bump into *her*."

Izzie shot a look at Rosalie. "What do you mean?" she said.

"Oh, nothing," said Rosalie. "C'mon, kiddo. Let's get you into bed. It's late."

It was 2:35 A.M. when Izzie and Joey woke up. The ceiling and walls of their room were fiery red with flickering, flashing light. Down by the water, they could hear sounds of small and large explosions going off. Izzie jumped out of bed and rushed out into the hall. "What *is* it?" she yelled, as her mother and Rosalie appeared at their own bedroom doors.

Rosalie had her hair done up in a bundle of curlers, with a red scarf tied around her head.

She was full of business, and different from the way she usually was. She wasn't singing and dancing. She was giving orders.

"Get your coats on," she said, in a deadly serious voice. "And we'd better warn some other people. I don't know what's going on, but I *do* know what's on that ship. We'll have to get out of here—and *fast.*"

Now Izzie could hear the low loud boom of guns. Whatever it was, it was real. It wasn't someone practising for anything. Had a ship or a submarine slipped through the harbour gates? The pit of her stomach felt empty with fear.

"Hurry!" cried Rosalie, as Mrs. Publicover struggled to get Joey into his coat. She almost yelled it. "And don't go near the windows! *There are enough explosives on that vessel to blow half of Dartmouth and Halifax off the map! I mean it!*"

Rosalie herded them all to the front door like a bunch of sheep. Mrs. Publicover had her arms around Izzie and Joey, but she was watching Rosalie carefully and doing everything she told them to do.

Outside, the noise from the explosions was deafening, the sky glowing and flashing. Rosalie faced the family, with her back to the road in front of the house. She looked like a huge monster, silhouetted against the red sky. Her big curlers and scarf made her head look like something that wasn't quite human.

"Listen to what I'm saying," she said, loud enough to be heard above the crackling explosions. "Bess, we're going to use my car, not the truck. Here are the keys. Open it up and get inside with Joey. Open the car windows. *Don't leave.* Izzie, you go over and wake up the Johnstones and Patricia, and tell them to get in their car and drive down towards Cow Bay. I'll go down and make sure Roberta's family knows what danger we're in, and warn them to keep away from the windows. Don't forget what happened to people's eyes in the Halifax Explosion."

She handed Mrs. Publicover the car keys and was off over the road and down towards the hill above Roberta's house. Izzie's mother pushed Joey into the car and yelled at Izzie.

"I have to stay with Joey. So *hurry!* I don't want you out there. Warn Patricia's family, and then get back here as fast as you can!"

But as Izzie started to run over to Patricia's house, she could see lights going on in all the houses. No one seemed to have remembered about the blackout curtains. As she approached the Johnstones', the door opened, and Patricia appeared in the doorway. She was in her pyjamas and bare feet, and she stood for a moment staring at the flashing lights, the gigantic streaks of fire, the red sky. The guns were steady now, filling the air with sounds like short bursts of thunder.

Suddenly, Patricia started to scream. She screamed and screamed, with both hands pulling at her hair. Then she moved out onto the road and began running. She started off in the direction of the harbour, flying across the field, sometimes running in circles, sometimes waving her arms around. She ran through the gravelly bits of land and through patches of snow in her bare feet, still screaming, screaming. Izzie, who was racing after her, could hear her above the noise of the guns. When she caught up with her at the edge of the hill overlooking the harbour, Patricia stopped screaming and stood stark still. They could see it all—the *Trongate,*

When Izzie caught up with
her at the edge of the hill
overlooking the harbour,
Patricia stopped screaming
and stood stark still.

the ship that was shooting at her, the blazing redness lighting up the night sky, the huge columns of flame flying out of her each time she was hit.

Patricia was now crying in dry heaving sobs. Izzie put an arm around her shoulder and held her tight.

"Listen to me, Patricia," she said, her voice steady but loud. "We have to get out of here before that ship blows up! Like right *now!* Take my hand and we'll tear back home. *C'mon!*" She grabbed Patricia's hand and started to run. Although that hand was now as limp as a fish, Patricia stumbled along after Izzie, as fast as she could. But that wasn't very fast.

Suddenly Rosalie was beside them. She picked up Patricia in her arms, and both she and Izzie ran towards the company houses, faster than they'd ever run before. When they came close to the car, Izzie's mother rushed out and hugged her so hard that Izzie thought she might break one of her ribs. Her mother was crying. Between gulps and sobs she was saying, "I couldn't … leave Joey … and I couldn't … chase you. I thought … I'd never see you again."

Rosalie cut in. "Get in the car. *Get in! Hurry!*" The Johnstones know we've got Patricia. Bess— take that big rug in the back seat and wrap her in it. Izzie—you sit beside them and rub her cold feet. Joey—you come in the front seat with me. All of you—keep your windows open!" Then she started the car, and they were off—headed for Cow Bay.

Rubbing Patricia's feet was a slithery business, but Izzie did it. Patricia had cut her bare feet so badly in that race across the road and fields that they were slippery with blood. Izzie took off her scarf—her favourite wool scarf, knit by her grandmother, with polar bears embroidered on it—and wrapped it round and round Patricia's feet. Then she laid them in her lap, under her coat. Her mother was holding Patricia in her arms like a baby, saying, "It's OK. It's OK," and stroking her cheek.

Izzie wiped her hands on her nightie, but they were still sticky. She didn't care. She was alive and so were a lot of other people. She'd seen them piling into their cars and leaving—including Roberta and her family. If the Nazis were attacking the *Trongate,* they might be able to attack both of the cities. Maybe they'd found a way to open the harbour gates and let in a lot of other ships and submarines, which could blow up the vessels in Bedford Basin and in the harbour.

It was scary, but the main thing that Izzie felt right now was *tired.* She felt safe in that back seat with her mother and Patricia. And Patricia was looking different from the person Izzie thought she knew. She was smiling quietly as Izzie's mother held her, and she looked calm and peaceful.

Patricia's eyes were drooping and she was very close to sleep. Izzie heard her say something very softly.

"What?"

"You didn't get angry," said Patricia. "No one was angry with me."

"Why would we be mad?" asked Izzie, puzzled.

"For screaming and crying. And running away. And going a little bit nuts."

Mrs. Publicover was still whispering, "It's OK. It's OK." Patricia looked up at her and grinned.

"Rosalie carried me, and you're hugging me," said Patricia's sleepy voice, "and my best friend wrapped up my freezing feet. I don't even mind them hurting. Or even the other things inside me that hurt." That was a long speech for Patricia, but as soon as she'd finished, she fell sound asleep.

A little bit nuts. That didn't sound like something the old Patricia would have said. Izzie looked at the new Patricia, sound asleep in her mother's arms, and thought, *I just knew there was another person inside her. I was just waiting for her to come out.* She gave Patricia's sore feet a small squeeze. Then she frowned. What did Patricia mean by "the other things inside me that hurt"? So there were still some mysteries to solve.

While they were driving towards Cow Bay, Izzie thought about how she'd love to tell her father about tonight's adventures. But when she tried to imagine that scene, her father had no face. She still couldn't remember what he looked like.

CHAPTER N°13

Rosalie and her four passengers spent what was left of the night—which was really the morning—at her Aunt Lucy's house at Cow Bay. Patricia's feet were bandaged up after she had a hot bath, but she was only half awake while it was happening. Then all of them were put to bed on couches and the one spare bed, wrapped up in Aunt Lucy's patchwork quilts.

Later that morning, Rosalie made a phone call to the sugar refinery and learned that it was safe to return to Woodside. She also discovered a lot of amazing things. On the way home, she told the others what she'd found out.

For some unknown reason, fire had broken out below decks on the *Trongate*. And Rosalie had been right. There'd been enough ammunition and explosives on the *Trongate* to blow up most of the two hundred ships at anchor in the harbour and half of the two cities. Later, when the fireboats and tugs failed to put out the fire, the Royal Canadian Navy minesweeper *Chedabucto* finally arrived, with orders to scuttle her—that is, to sink and destroy her—before the ship blew up and created a second catastrophic Halifax Explosion. For forty-five minutes the *Chedabucto* fired sand-filled four-inch shells precisely at the waterline of the burning ship, praying that the impact of the dead shells wouldn't cause the very explosion they were trying to avoid. With each shot, a giant pillar of flame shot skyward from the burning ship—which is exactly what they had all seen the night before.

After twenty-three rounds of shells were fired, the *Trongate* gradually leaned to one side and sank in seventy-six feet of water at 3:25 in the morning. She'd been on fire below decks and calling for help since ten o'clock on the previous evening. *What had caused such an appalling delay?*

Izzie could hardly believe what she was hearing. She'd been so sure that people would be too smart in 1942 to let another huge explosion take place. And it had been so very, very close to happening.

On Saturday of the next week, Izzie set aside a whole morning to write to Jasper.

She hadn't written for a long time, and she had a lot of things she wanted to tell him. Of course, she told him about the *Trongate* and how close death had seemed. In fact, how close death *was*. That took most of the morning. In the afternoon, she wrote some more.

Dear Jasper again,

Now I have two almost-best friends. Patricia has loosened up since her screaming fit, and now she knows how to cry and to laugh and to sort of forget who she's trying to be. Most of the time anyway. And maybe to get to know her real self.

But don't worry. You're still my very best friend. I miss Granite Cove. I wish you lived here, and I wish Clementine could come and have her own little private barn in our backyard. Please go over and give her some loving pats. Tell her they're from me.

The best thing I have to tell you is that this morning Mum got a phone call from GUESS WHO? DAD! *His ship is in Bedford Basin, and this afternoon he's coming home here to spend five days with us. It could happen any minute. I wonder if I'll remember what he looks like. I'm scared out of my wits that I won't. I'm so excited that I feel like the top of my head might fly right off.*

Mum is downstairs preparing Dad's favourite food. Rosalie is helping her. Roast chicken. French fries. Pressed cucumbers. Sauerkraut. Joey is making him a Welcome Home card. I just finished knitting a navy blue scarf for him yesterday. It has a few mistakes, and the knitting is kind of tight in places, but it'll be

warm, and he'll know I made it. It took me two and
a half months. Of course, I wasn't working on it every
single minute. But even so. And now I won't have to
send it by mail or have to worry that some submarine
might torpedo it out of existence.

If you want me to make you a scarf, let me know.
Say what colour you want. I think I could do stripes,
if you'd like that.

Your friend,
Izzie Publicover

Izzie put her pen down and looked out the
window. Maybe she'd go and skip with Roberta
or Patricia while she was waiting. Or perhaps
play hopscotch on the dirt path. She looked
along the road towards the Johnstones' house.

There he was, at the end of the long string of
company houses, getting out of a car. There
were the sailor hat, the navy pea jacket, the bell-
bottom trousers. And there, when he turned
around, was his face. *She'd know him anywhere.* In

the Sahara Desert. In the jungles of Africa. At the North Pole. How could she have thought she'd forgotten what he looked like?

It was a cold and windy April day. There were snowflakes in the air. But Izzie raced down the stairs and out the door without her rubbers or coat or kerchief. She ran, ran, as fast as she could run to the end of the road, where her father was waiting. He'd put his duffle bag on the ground and was holding his arms wide open. She took a running jump and flew right into them.

AUTHOR'S NOTE

From what I have read about the *Trongate* incident, it is impossible for me to answer the question you read on page 94 of *Trongate Fury:* "What had caused such an appalling delay?"

Certainly, several factors contributed to the length of time that passed before the vessel was scuttled. But they fail to satisfy me completely.

It is true that April 9 had been a day of unusual activity and disorder in Halifax Harbour. It had been rumoured that a submarine had slipped through the gate that protected the harbour from the outer sea. Therefore, there was a lot of movement as ships' crews tried to discover if this were true. The harbour also contained the second-largest number of ships since the start of the war. Thousands of German prisoners had arrived that day on the *Rangatiki,* and two other ships had been loading troops, who now awaited a convoy to take them overseas. That evening, there was a great deal of noise, as well as confusion with Aldis lamp signals. With the amount of submarine activity that existed just outside the harbour's gate, SOS signals were not at all uncommon. And on McNab's Island and at Maugers

Beach, two beached ships were smouldering from their own recent fires. The *Trongate*'s commander was also indecisive as to whether the ship should be beached or sunk. And, most important, there seems to have been extremely poor communication among naval, military, and civilian authorities.

Shortly after receiving word at 10 P.M. that the *Trongate* was on fire and carrying TNT, fireboats and tugs were sent out to try to quell the fire with their hoses. But for several hours, the fire below decks continued to be hard to locate, and therefore almost impossible to extinguish. When the *Chedabucto* was finally called on to come and scuttle the burning ship, it took a significant amount of time for them to load the necessary ammunition—shells filled with sand, in order to minimize the danger of explosion. When the *Chedabucto* arrived and started firing its guns—slowly and carefully, exactly at the waterline—citizens in Dartmouth and Halifax called the phone company to ask for explanations. The phone operators incredibly reported that "a burning ship is being sunk by gunfire and there is no danger."

Because of the complexity of signals and messages, people who lived close to the harbour were never evacuated. It would seem that neither the civilian police nor the air-raid wardens tried to make this happen. None of the ships in the harbour—including those close to the burning ship—hauled up their anchors and moved away.

The crews of two hundred vessels and the population of two cities were in the kind of peril that is difficult to assess or describe. There were people who knew about the deadly cargo that the *Trongate* had on board. Why would anyone think that fire boats and small tugs could do enough to prevent a catastrophic explosion? Reasons have been given as to why it took so long to scuttle the *Trongate*. But they do not lessen my shock—nor my anger—over that long delay. Halifax is my own city, and I was there at the time. I remember well the terrifying sound of those guns during the long hour it took the *Chedabucto* to succeed in its mission.

Dear Reader,

Welcome back to the continuing adventures of Our Canadian Girl! It's been another exciting year for us here at Penguin, publishing new stories and continuing the adventures of twelve terrrific girls. The best part of this past year, though, has been the wonderful letters we've received from readers like you, telling us your favourite Our Canadian Girl story and which parts you liked the most. Best of all, you told us which stories you would like to read, and we were amazed! There are so many remarkable stories in Canadian history. It seems that wherever we live, great stories live there too, in our towns and cities, on our rivers and mountains. Thank you so much for sharing them.

So please, stay in touch. Write letters, log on to our website, let us know what you think of Our Canadian Girl. We're listening.

Sincerely,
Barbara Berson

1608
Samuel de
Champlain
establishes
the first
fortified
trading post
at Quebec.

1759
The British
defeat the
French in
the Battle
of the
Plains of
Abraham.

1812
The United
States
declares war
against
Canada.

1845
The expedition of
Sir John Franklin
to the Arctic ends
when the ship is
frozen in the pack
ice; the fate of its
crew remains a
mystery.

1869
Louis Riel
leads his
Métis
followers in
the Red
River
Rebellion.

1871
British
Columbia
joins
Canada.

1755
The British
expel the
entire French
population
of Acadia
(today's
Maritime
provinces),
sending
them into
exile.

1776
The 13
Colonies
revolt
against
Britain, and
the Loyalists
flee to
Canada.

1837
Calling for
responsible
government, the
Patriotes, following
Louis-Joseph
Papineau, rebel in
Lower Canada;
William Lyon
Mackenzie leads the
uprising in Upper
Canada.

1867
New
Brunswick,
Nova Scotia
and the United
Province of
Canada come
together in
Confederation
to form the
Dominion of
Canada.

1870
Manitoba joins
Canada. The
Northwest
Territories
become an
official
territory of
Canada.

1783
Rachel

1865
Angelique

1885
At Craigellachie, British Columbia, the last spike is driven to complete the building of the Canadian Pacific Railway.

1898
The Yukon Territory becomes an official territory of Canada.

1914
Britain declares war on Germany, and Canada, because of its ties to Britain, is at war too.

1918
As a result of the Wartime Elections Act, the women of Canada are given the right to vote in federal elections.

1945
World War II ends conclusively with the dropping of atomic bombs on Hiroshima and Nagasaki.

1873
Prince Edward Island joins Canada.

1896
Gold is discovered on Bonanza Creek, a tributary of the Klondike River.

1905
Alberta and Saskatchewan join Canada.

1917
In the Halifax harbour, two ships collide, causing an explosion that leaves more than 1,600 dead and 9,000 injured.

1939
Canada declares war on Germany seven days after war is declared by Britain and France.

1949
Newfoundland, under the leadership of Joey Smallwood, joins Canada.

1942
Izzie

1944
Margit

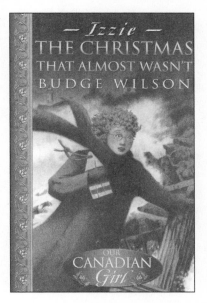